5-MINUTE

Disney

VILLAINS

STORIES

Disney PRESS

Los Angeles • New York

CONTENTS

COUP AT THE ZOO

"What?" Cruella barked into her phone late one night.

A smooth voice came over the line. "Ma'am, Horace is the name. Me and my best mate, Jasper, here would be honored to be your humble crooks."

Cruella grinned. Not the type to get her hands dirty, but with much dirty work to do, she had put an ad in the paper in hopes of finding henchmen. It appeared she had her first candidates.

"Splendid. Meet me tomorrow at the local inn. Eight o'clock. *Sharp.*"

The next night, Cruella sped off to interview the two hopefuls. As she scanned the room, a ruckus erupted.

"It was *my* smarts we used to scam this hot meal, and for some reason it's in *your* mouth."

"You wouldn't know smarts if they fell from the sky and hit you on your big head!"

Cruella smiled, recognizing one of the voices.

Cruella walked over to the bickering men. "Enough," she said, and right away they both fell silent.

"Darlings, I'm Cruella De Vil. A pleasure, I'm sure. If you'd like to become my new . . . assistants . . . you must convince me you're a good fit. I'd like for you to steal an animal from the new zoo. Can you do it?" She jangled her purse for added effect, and the crooks eyed it with wild hunger.

"Just tell us when and we'll be there," Jasper said. Horace nodded along eagerly.

"Excellent. We meet tomorrow at dusk at Regent's Park."

The next evening, Cruella met Horace and Jasper outside the soon-to-open London Zoo. "Get in there, and quickly!"

"Yes, ma'am! Which animal do you fancy we fetch for you, Miss Dev—Miss De Vil?" Horace hollered.

"Not so loud!" Cruella scolded. "That one!" She jabbed her finger at a newspaper photo of a polar bear.

"This'll be easy, ma'am," whispered Jasper. "Like taking babies from a candy." He nodded confidently. "Be right back."

"All right, now, easy does it. . . ." Jasper guided Horace, who was working a large net into the sleeping polar bear's cage. But it turned out the animal was in no mood to be bear-napped.

"You just *had* to wake it up, didn't you?" Jasper shouted at Horace as they made a hasty retreat.

"Well, you wasn't exactly quiet yourself!" Horace shot back.

Cruella turned crimson when she saw the duo without her promised prize. "You . . . *cowards*!" she sputtered.

"Ah, we're sorry, ma'am," Horace said. "What about a smaller animal? A cheetah, perhaps?"

Cruella glared at them. Finally, she sighed. "I do have a soft spot for, well, *spots*." She cackled, then quickly scowled at the two men. "All right. A cheetah. And I'm coming with you this time to make sure you don't mess this up."

But the cheetah was too fast for the slow-witted crooks. And when Horace and Jasper failed to steal a lion next, Cruella grew even more furious.

When they failed at thieving an elephant, Cruella's eye began to twitch.

It seemed clear as day that Horace and Jasper did not have what it took to crook.

But Cruella was willing to give them one final shot. "Try stealing one of the more docile little beasts," she instructed them. "Do it, and do it now!"

Horace and Jasper wasted no time breaking into the children's petting zoo.

"We've got this one in the can, mate," Jasper said to Horace as they sauntered into the animal pens.

But then . . . the baby llamas spit in their faces.

The piglets chased them into the mud.

And the ducklings pecked at them in the pond.

Outside the petting zoo, Cruella was growing more and more impatient. Suddenly, the men appeared. And they ran right past her.

"Stampede!" yelled Jasper.

"Run!" shouted Horace.

Cruella craned her neck to see the massive beasts that had inspired such terror in her would-be underlings. But all that scampered into view were fuzzy ducklings, muddy piglets, sweet baby llamas, and bleating baby goats!

Cruella boiled over, realizing that Horace and Jasper must have accidentally released the petting zoo animals. *"Idiots!"* she yelled.

She'd had enough of Horace and Jasper's hijinks. "You complete imbeciles!" she shouted as they ran past her again. She looked around. What an utter disaster.

Were these really the best henchmen she could find? Cruella would have to do everything herself!

One beastly animal she could have gotten away with—but she didn't want the police on high alert because someone had stolen the entire children's petting zoo!

"I'll handle this," she grumbled. She retrieved her car and corralled all the animals back into their cages and pens . . .

. . . eventually.

"My car! It's filthy! You are good for nothing! You can't even clean up your own mess! Didn't I mention I hate getting my hands dirty?" Cruella roared at Horace and Jasper. "This is the *last* time I ever work with you . . . you . . ."

"Idiots?" Horace suggested.

"Complete imbeciles?" Jasper offered.

"Shut up!" Cruella screamed. The men flinched. Cruella was fuming. She stomped off into the night. Horace and Jasper looked at each other and shrugged, thinking of how they could make it up to Cruella.

A little while later, Cruella sagged up the stairs to her room at the manor.

She opened the door, and her jaw dropped: her bedroom had been completely transformed! The furniture had all been uncovered, and everything sparkled like new.

Just then, there was a tap on her door.

Horace and Jasper were standing in the hallway. "Now you don't have to get your hands any dirtier than they are!" Horace burst out, triumphant.

"We can't fix up our own messes, but we sure could fix up yours, ma'am!" added Jasper.

"You did, didn't you. . . . Well, you did a rather mediocre job." But
Cruella couldn't fight the smile. "It is kind of nice to have company here.
It can get a bit lonely. Okay, fine, I'll have you two as my assistants."

Horace and Jasper cheered as Cruella flopped down on her newly
made bed, dirt and all. "Now, let's see if your bacon is better than your
thieving."

THE CURSE OF THE CROW

There was nothing Smee hated more than gathering firewood—not even swabbing the decks! But Captain Hook had given him his orders.

Smee was wandering through the woods when he smelled smoke. He chuckled. "If somebody's gathered wood for a bonfire, they've done the work for me!"

In a nearby clearing, Smee found Peter Pan, Tinker Bell, Wendy, John, and Michael sitting around a crackling fire.

"Tell us a scary story, Wendy," Peter Pan said.

A sly smile crossed Wendy's face. "Have you ever heard of the Curse of the Crow?" she asked.

The boys shook their heads.

"Long ago there lived a wise old crow," Wendy began. "Though he was wise, he envied the cleverness of people. Since he could not compete with them, he cursed them instead!

"There were four signs that you had been cursed," Wendy continued. "First there would be bird tracks. Then soot in the soap. And sudden fits of *sneezing*. But worst of all . . ."

"What? What was worst?" the boys chorused.

"A single black feather would appear on your pillow," Wendy said. "That meant that the crow had *cursed you for life!*"

Just then, a *caw-caw-caw!* rang through the clearing.

Everyone around the bonfire jumped. Smee, who was hiding in the bushes, was so scared that his knees started knocking together! He grabbed the nearest pile of twigs and skedaddled all the way back to the *Jolly Roger*.

"Oh, Peter," Wendy said with a laugh. "That was a perfectly timed *caw*, I should say!"

Peter grinned. He had noticed Smee hiding in the bushes and thought to give him a good scare. He was sure the pirate would be shaking for the rest of the night!

"I'll put out the fire," Peter said, as it was getting close to bedtime.

As he splashed a pail of water onto the bonfire, Peter had an idea. He beckoned to John and Tink. "I know how to teach that Smee a lesson once and for all," he began. "But first we'll need a pine branch, some flowers, and all this soggy soot. . . ."

Meanwhile, Smee had made it back to the *Jolly Roger*. "Captain! Captain!" he cried breathlessly as he ran onto the ship.

"What is it? The Crocodile?" Captain Hook shrieked, jumping.

"No," Smee replied. "It's the Curse of the Crow!" He told the crew Wendy's story, but none of the other pirates were scared.

"Why, there ain't never been a crow in Never Land!" one of the pirates jeered.

"But I heard one," Smee protested.

While Smee was telling the pirates Wendy's story, Peter Pan, Tink, and John snuck onto the *Jolly Roger*.

Peter whispered, "Tink—you're up!"

Tink dipped a pine sprig into the pail of wet soot. Then she flew around the ship, leaving dirty marks that looked just like bird tracks!

When Smee saw the marks, he gasped. "Bird tracks!" he exclaimed. "It's the Curse of the Crow!"

But Captain Hook did not believe in the curse.

He just saw a big mess. "You call this shipshape?" he bellowed at his crew. "Swab the decks at once, or you'll walk the plank!"

Smee scrambled to add soap powder to pails of water. "They'll see," he grumbled. "The curse is real!"

"Your turn, John," Peter whispered. "Hurry!"

When Smee's back was turned, John dashed forward and sprinkled soot into the pails. When the pirates started mopping the deck, they made the mess even worse!

"Oh, *no,*" Smee moaned, hiding his eyes. "The crow's curse is happening, just the way Wendy said it would!"

"A cursed ship's not fit to sail," one of the pirates said.

"The only curse you have to worry about is from *me* if you don't clean this up!" Captain Hook growled.

"Now, Tink!" Peter whispered. Tinker Bell grabbed the bunch of flowers and flew high into the air. Then she shook the flowers, sprinkling pollen all over the pirates!

"Nice clean soap, turned black and murky as mud," one of the pirates said. "Something strange is afoot!"

"Yes," Hook muttered. "I—ah-ah-*achoo!*"

"Sneezing!" gasped Smee. "The next stage of the crow's curse!"

But the pirates were sneezing so loudly that no one could even hear him!

"We—*achoo!*—are—*achoo!*—doomed!" Smee howled between sneezes.

"Now see here," Captain Hook said when his sneezing fit finally died down. "There is *no* Curse of the Crow. This is more like the work of a rascal!"

"What do you mean, Captain?" Smee asked.

"Peter Pan is trying to make fools of us all," Hook explained. "Search the ship and seize that scoundrel!"

"Aye, aye, Captain!" the pirates yelled.

"That's our cue," Peter told the others. "Away we go!"

"Captain! Look!" Smee said in astonishment as he spotted two figures flying past the full moon.

"What did I tell you?" Captain Hook gloated, pushing past Smee and making his way toward his cabin. "I knew there would be an explanation for all this silliness."

"You were right, Captain," Smee said, breathing a sigh of relief. "It was just Peter Pan. After all, it's not like anyone found a crow's feather on his pillow. Now *that* would be really scary. Imagine being cursed . . . for life!"

"You imagine it," Captain Hook retorted. "I'm going to bed."

Captain Hook took his key and unlocked the door to his cabin. "Cursed for life," he said with a chuckle as he lit a candle. "Poppycock!"

Then he saw it: a single dark feather, right on his pillow! Captain Hook's face grew very pale. "P-P-Peter P-P-Pan?" he stammered. But how? The cabin had been locked, and Captain Hook had already seen him fly away!

Perhaps the Curse of the Crow was real after all!

SHADOWS IN THE JUNGLE

There was one animal in the jungle whom all the others feared: Shere Khan. The tiger was ferocious and very scary. The animals tried to keep their distance from him. And they stuck together because there was safety in numbers.

One sunny day in the jungle, the Dawn Patrol was on its afternoon march. Colonel Hathi marched at the front of the line. His son brought up the rear.

"Hup, two, three, four!" the elephants chanted.

As the patrol marched through a row of flowering trees, Colonel Hathi's trunk began to twitch. Then it wiggled. Then . . .

"Achooooo!" The colonel sneezed, jerking backward. He bumped into the elephant behind him. That elephant bumped into the next elephant, and *that* elephant into the one behind him. The elephants kept bumping into each other until . . .

Bam! The last elephant bumped into Hathi's son. The little elephant tumbled backward into a large hole in the ground.

Thump! The baby elephant landed in a heap. He blinked and looked around. He was in a cave. Spiders and strange bugs skittered up the walls and across the floor. In front of him, the wind whipped eerily through several dark tunnels.

The elephant didn't know which way to go. He couldn't be sure which of the tunnels would lead him out of the cave, and they all looked so scary!

"Heeeeeelp!" he cried. The elephant's voice echoed through the cave. But the Dawn Patrol had already marched on. They didn't hear the little elephant's call for help.

Across the jungle, Shere Khan's ears twitched.

"That sounds like the cry of a helpless animal," the tiger purred in his deep voice. "Music to my ears!"

Shere Khan swiftly made his way toward the sound, his padded feet moving silently across the jungle floor.

Hanging in the nearby trees, three monkeys heard the elephant's call for help, too.

"What's that?" the first monkey asked.

"Let's go see!" the second monkey said.

The monkeys swung from branch to branch, heading toward the noise. But they stopped when they saw Shere Khan.

"Never mind!" the third monkey whispered. "Let's get out of here!"

On the ground below, Mowgli and Baloo were having fun rolling down a hill.

"Hey!" Mowgli called out as the monkeys swung past them. "What's the hurry?"

The monkeys stopped.

"We didn't hear anything!" the first monkey shouted.

"We didn't see anything, either!" the second monkey yelled.

"That's right," said the third monkey. "We definitely did not hear a little elephant call out for help or see Shere Khan making his way toward the sound."

Mowgli jumped up. "A little elephant? Hathi's son is in trouble!"

"Which way did you not hear a little elephant call for help?" Baloo asked.

The monkeys all pointed over their shoulders, and Baloo and Mowgli ran off to help their friend.

Meanwhile, back in the cave, the light was beginning to fade. The poor baby elephant stared at the tunnels.

"I'm sure the Dawn Patrol will be here any minute to rescue me," he told himself.

The little elephant shivered. A strange feeling came over him . . . a feeling that he wasn't alone in the cave anymore.

Suddenly, two large yellow eyes appeared in one of the dark tunnels. The little elephant froze with fear as Shere Khan stepped out of the darkness.

"Good afternoon," the tiger said, his eyes fixed on the elephant.

Mowgli and Baloo heard the elephant's cry. They raced toward the sound as fast as they could. They soon came to a cave in the side of a rocky cliff.

"He must be in there," Mowgli said, starting forward, but Baloo stopped him.

"Look there, little buddy," the bear said.

He pointed to some fresh paw prints leading into the cave. Tiger paw prints!

"We've got to do something," Mowgli said, determined to help his friend. He looked at the cave. He saw the last rays of the setting sun starting to fade.

"Hmmm," Mowgli said, scratching his chin. "I've got an idea, but I'll need your help."

Inside the cave, Shere Khan grinned slyly at the elephant.

"Your father and his elephant patrol are quite fierce," the tiger murmured in his deep, smooth voice. "But you, little one, are another story. You shall make quite a tasty morsel."

The baby elephant gulped. What would his pop do?

"You won't eat me!" he said, trying to look as brave as he could. "The Dawn Patrol will rescue me!"

Shere Khan shook his head. "They're long gone," he said. "Now let us finish this."

The tiger moved forward but then stopped. Shadows had started to flicker on the wall. The little elephant saw Shere Khan's scared face and turned around to look.

"Men!" the elephant cried. "Men with torches!"

Nothing frightened Shere Khan more than Man and his fire. The tiger growled. "Our dinner engagement will have to wait, I'm afraid," he said. And with that, he raced out of the cave.

Hidden from sight, Mowgli and Baloo watched the frightened tiger sprint into the jungle.

When they were sure Shere Khan was gone, Mowgli and Baloo stepped into the cave.

"Are you all right?" Mowgli asked.

"I'm fine!" the elephant called.

Mowgli ran to his friend and hugged him. "Don't worry about Shere Khan," he said. "We got rid of him."

"But where are the men and their torches?" the elephant asked.

Baloo held up some leaves. "Just a little trick of the light!"

The three friends set off through the tunnel that led back into the jungle. They came out of the cave just in time to see the Dawn Patrol marching toward them.

"Pop!" the little elephant cried, running up to his father. "I fell into a cave, and Shere Khan almost got me, but Mowgli and Baloo saved me."

"Thank you, both," Colonel Hathi said. "I am in your debt."

Mowgli grinned. "That's what friends are for!"

ALICE in WONDERLAND

QUEEN of FRIGHTS

"Where are we going again?" Alice asked the Mad Hatter as they dashed through Wonderland together.

"'Where' isn't the right question," the Mad Hatter said.

"Well then, what *is* the right question?" Alice asked, confused.

"Not *what*. Why?" the Mad Hatter replied. "*What* we are doing is having fun. You should ask me *why* we are going."

Alice shook her head. Wonderland logic was a bit confusing, but she was finally getting the hang of it. "Very well," she said. *"Why* are we going?"

"I don't know why," the Mad Hatter answered. "I just know that we are in a hurry!"

The Mad Hatter rushed along, and a curious Alice followed. The sky grew dark, and fat raindrops began to fall.

The Mad Hatter plucked a flower and handed it to her. "A little rain never hurt anyone. Here, use this!"

Nearby, at the castle, the Queen of Hearts was feeling quite cranky. She had not slept well the night before and was in need of a good, long nap.

"If anyone disturbs me, I will have their head!" she barked at the guards as she stomped into her royal chamber.

Spotting the rain streaming in through her open window, the Queen frowned.

"Nasty rain," she muttered. Then she took off her crown, placed it gently on the table beside her, and climbed into bed.

In no time at all, the Queen of Hearts was sound asleep. But the Queen was not a quiet sleeper, and she was soon snoring so loudly that she woke herself up! When she opened her eyes, she saw that the table beside her was empty.

"My crown!" she cried, jumping out of bed.

The Queen of Hearts looked around frantically. Finally, she spotted

"This is some kind of trick!" the Queen said. Then she raised her voice so that everyone could hear her. "Whoever is trying to trick me will LOSE THEIR HEAD!"

The Queen climbed back into bed and closed her eyes. But a strange noise filled the room. *Creeeeeak . . . creeeeeak . . . creeeeeak . . .*

"What *is* that racket?" she cried, sitting up.

Then she saw her rocking chair swaying back and forth . . . back and forth. . . .

"*Hmph!* It must be a breeze," the Queen told herself. But the window and the shutters were closed tight—just as she had left them. Something else was moving the chair!

"Who's there?" the Queen yelled. She tried to sound threatening, but her voice was beginning to shake. She stomped across the room and stopped the rocking chair from rocking. Then she climbed into

The Queen of Hearts closed her eyes. She had just started to snore when a new noise woke her up!

Squeeeak . . . squeeeak . . . squeeeak . . .

The Queen bolted upright in bed. She saw the doors to her wardrobe swinging wide open. The hinges were making an eerie squeaking sound.

"Wh-whoever is t-t-tricking me will l-l-lose th-th-their h-h-head," the Queen whispered in fright. She ran up and closed the wardrobe doors. Then she turned to go back to bed.

Creeeeeak . . . creeeeeak . . . creeeeeak . . .

The Queen spun around. Something had come out of the wardrobe! It had legs but no feet. It had arms but no hands. And worst of all, it had no head!

"Aaaaaaaaaaah!" the Queen of Hearts screamed. "A GHOST!"

Alice and the Mad Hatter had just arrived outside the castle when they heard the Queen's screams.

"Oh, my. Is this where we are?" the Mad Hatter said. "Here is *not*

As Alice turned to follow the Mad Hatter, she spotted something on the ground. "I think I know *why* we are doing what we are doing," she said. "We need to go inside that castle."

They crept into the Queen's castle.

A few moments later, Alice and the Mad Hatter burst into the Queen's chamber.

"Ghost! Ghost!" the Queen of Hearts yelled. She was as white as a sheet and trembling from head to toe.

Alice marched up to the ghost and pulled off its shirt. It was the March Hare! The little Dormouse peeked out of the front pocket of the March Hare's jacket.

"I remember now!" the Mad Hatter cried. "We were playing hide-and-seek!"

"We were looking for a place to hide," the March Hare said, "but nowhere seemed to work. The crown was too small, the chair was too creaky, and the wardrobe was too stuffy!"

The Queen of Hearts turned a deep shade of red. "OFF WITH YOUR HEADS!" she screamed.

The Mad Hatter knew when it was time to go. He tapped the March Hare on the shoulder. "You're it!" he cried. Then he ran off.

Alice followed him. The palace guards chased after her.

"Off with their heads!" the Queen of Hearts screamed again.

Outside, the rain had stopped. But fortunately, the ground was wet. The guards slipped and slid, giving Alice and her friends a chance to get away.

Back in the Mad Hatter's garden, Alice and her friends enjoyed a nice cup of tea.

"That was fun!" the Mad Hatter exclaimed.

The March Hare agreed. "Let's play another game," he said.

"What do you say, Alice?" the Mad Hatter asked.

"I think I've had enough games for one day," Alice replied. "I'm quite fond of my head, and I'd like to keep it!"

Disney

Peter Pan

A TRICK FOR HOOK

The weather in Never Land was the same as it always was: warm and breezy. Perfect for Wendy Darling to practice her flying. She was hovering unsteadily several feet above the ground when she remembered what day it was.

"Oh!" Wendy cried. She lost her concentration and fell to the ground with an *oof.*

"Why, it's All Hallows' Eve," she said, standing up and dusting herself off.

"What's that?" Peter asked.

"It's a holiday with all kinds of spooky things," Wendy explained. "And some not-so-spooky things, too. Like bobbing for apples."

"And turnips!" John added. "Tell him about the turnips, Wendy!"

"Oh, yes," Wendy said. "You hollow out a turnip and give it a face—"

"And put a candle inside!" Michael finished.

"That sounds *boring,*" Peter declared rudely.

Wendy thought it over. "Well, *I* don't think it's boring," she said.
"You know, they say that All Hallows' Eve is the night that all the
ghosts come out!"

Peter's eyes widened. Now that was interesting to him. "I *love*
ghosts!" he cried. "Are they *scary* ghosts?"

Wendy nodded gravely. "On All Hallows' Eve," she said in a
whisper, "the bats stay home. The owls hide in their trees. Even the
spiders are afraid to show their faces. That's how scary the ghosts are."

Peter shivered. "That's spooky," he said. He examined his arms.
"Look, I've got goose bumps."

The children all piled into Peter's hideout as Wendy continued describing All Hallows' Eve.

"People play tricks on each other on All Hallows' Eve," she said, "and tell spooky stories."

"Like what?" asked Peter.

"Well, there was a story Papa used to tell us about a haunted turnip," Wendy said. "It gave me nightmares!"

Peter looked thoughtful. In fact, he looked like he was hatching a brilliant scheme.

"Tricks," he said, pacing back and forth. "Spooky stories. Nightmares."

Then he flew straight up to the ceiling, so fast he almost hit his head.

"I've got it!" Peter said. "We'll play an All Hallows' Eve trick on Captain Hook!"

Peter dug around under the Lost Boys' hammocks. Finally, he found what he was looking for: an old white sheet and a tattered pirate hat.

"If there's one thing Captain Hook is afraid of," Peter said, "it's the crocodile who ate his hand. But if there's one thing all pirates fear, it's the ghost of the Old Sea Dog."

"Who's that?" Wendy asked.

"He's from a scary story pirates tell each other," Peter said, "a legend. He was supposed to have been the wickedest and cruelest of them all."

Peter tossed the sheet over his head and tossed the pirate hat over that.

"We're going to make Captain Hook think that the ghost of the Old Sea Dog is haunting Never Land this All Hallows' Eve," he said.

"Wooooooooooooooo," Peter added in a high, spooky tone. "Shiver me timbers!"

Wendy shuddered. She knew Peter was under there, but it was still a bit scary!

Peter, Tinker Bell, Wendy, and the boys snuck down to the beach as quietly as they could. Evening had fallen, and they stuck to the shadows as they went. When they reached the water, Tinker Bell sprinkled Wendy and the boys with pixie dust. The group rose into the air, gliding silently above the waves. Soon they had reached the *Jolly Roger*.

"Shhhh," Peter whispered as they flew around to the wheel, where Hook stood.

The night air was still, and the sound of the ocean lapping at the sides of
the ship was faint. Wendy, Peter, and the boys hovered silently in the shadow
of the ship, breathing as quietly as they could manage.

Aboard the *Jolly Roger*, Hook shifted from one foot to the other. The
shuffle of his bootheel on the deck was eerily loud.

"All Hallows' Eve," Hook muttered to himself. "I hate All Hallows' Eve."

"What's that, Cap'n?" came a jaunty—and unexpected—response from the shadows.

Hook jumped a mile in the air.

"Smee!" he yelled. "Don't sneak up on me like that!"

"Sorry, Cap'n," Smee said. "I forgot how you hate All Hallows' Eve."

"It's bad enough having that crocodile skulking around," Hook whined. "Now I have to watch out for ghosts on top of it?"

Hidden from sight, Peter winked at Wendy.

"Woooooooo," Peter moaned softly, still hidden at the side of the ship.

"What's that?" Captain Hook called sharply.

"Wooooooooooooooo," Peter added, a little louder.

"Who's there?" cried Smee.

"It is I," Peter said. He rose quickly to the deck, his sheet fluttering in the ocean wind. "The Oooooold Sea Dooooooog!"

He flew straight at Hook, moaning and screeching.

"Odsbodikins!" Hook screamed, and flung himself to the deck.

Laughing, the children fled as fast as they could. The look on
Hook's face had been priceless.

"Where's Peter?" Wendy asked when she and her brothers landed
on the beach.

The boys looked around, but Peter was nowhere to be found.

"Let's get home," Wendy suggested. "Maybe he'll meet us there."

But as they approached Peter's hideout, the hair on the back
of Wendy's neck began to stand up. They could see an eerie glow
through the trees. A glow like . . .

"*Boo!*"

Wendy gasped as a ghastly face appeared in front of them. A grinning head with no body, it bobbed and staggered through the air.

It was . . . *a floating turnip?*

"I tricked you!" crowed someone with a familiar voice.

Peter stepped out of the shadows, laughing so hard he was clutching his sides. Next to him hung the turnip, attached to a string.

Wendy sighed. "Peter, you really frightened me!" she scolded him. "But it was a good trick," she added.

"That was the idea!" he said. "After all, it's All Hallows' Eve! Why settle for one scare when you can get *two*?"

THE QUEEN'S SPELL

IT was a beautiful fall day. Everyone in the kingdom was happily enjoying the crisp air and the bright orange and red leaves on the trees. Everyone, that is, except for the Queen.

"Where are the gloomy gray clouds?" She scowled as she watched some children playing in a pile of fallen leaves. "Where is the cold autumn rain? Where are the fierce howling winds?"

Frustrated, the Queen stormed to her chambers to consult her Magic Mirror.

"Magic Mirror on the wall, when will I see a gloomy fall?" she asked. Purple smoke swirled, and a face appeared inside the mirror.

"Alas," the Magic Mirror replied, "I fear I see nothing but sunny skies."

"No rain? Not a gray cloud to be found? How can anyone stand all the cheer and happiness out there?" the Queen cried.

"Perhaps a spell could bring the gloom you seek," the Magic Mirror suggested.

"Of course!" the Queen said. "I shall use magic to chase away this cheerful weather."

The Queen hurried down the stairs to her secret chamber. It was full of dusty old books and bottles of potions. She picked up one of her spell books.

"Gray . . . gloom . . ." she muttered as she flipped through the pages. Then she stopped. "Here it is! A spell for a frightful day."

The Queen read the list of ingredients out loud. "Three spiders, for gray skies and rain. Two rats' whiskers, for howling winds. And five shimmering scales from a snake, for thunder and lightning. . . ."

The Queen pulled jar after jar from her shelves. Each one was empty. She had cast too many spells recently. She fumed, slamming an empty jar against the floor.

"I suppose I shall have to gather more," the Queen told herself. "Now, where would one find three spiders?"

The Queen's green eyes flashed as the answer came to her. "Of course! The well!"

The Queen marched upstairs, her cape swirling behind her. She pushed open the castle doors and stepped outside.

"Horrible sun!" she said, frowning at the bright sky.

The Queen's mood lightened as she reached the well. She was, after all, quite fond of spiders. "Where are you, my lovelies?" she asked, peering into the depths. "You love the dark dampness of the well

The Queen searched the well, but she did not see any spiders. Instead, she found three ladybugs hanging from the bucket, getting a drink of water.

The Queen's face darkened. "So tiny! So cute!" she thundered.

Frightened, the three ladybugs quickly flew off.

As the Queen walked away, she didn't notice the single gray cloud that floated into the sky overhead.

Grumbling, the Queen looked at her list. "Rats!" she said. "That is what I need to find. A nice messy rat's nest with a rat inside."

At the edge of the woods, the Queen spotted an old oak tree. A pile of straw was sticking out from its gnarled roots. She walked to the tree and knelt down.

"Where are you, my lovely rats?" she asked. "Are you huddled here inside this messy nest? Come out and offer me your whiskers."

The Queen pushed aside the straw. But she did not see any rats. Instead, she saw two baby chipmunks taking a nap!

The Queen's face darkened. "So sweet! So cuddly!" she thundered.

At the sound of her voice, the baby chipmunks awoke. They quickly scampered out of the nest and up the tree trunk. As the Queen stormed off, another gray cloud appeared in the sky.

Curses! I shall never finish this spell!" the Queen complained. "The Magic Mirror will pay for sending me on this foolish errand."

As she started to head back toward the castle, the Queen spotted a hole in the ground.

A snake's den!" she said hopefully, and stopped. "Come on out, lovely snake. I need some of your scales."

A creature poked out its head. But it wasn't a snake. It was a bunny rabbit!

"So fluffy! So soft!" the Queen shouted, and the terrified bunny hopped away.

Angry, the Queen lifted her arms to the sky. "I can't find anything I need. Everything is too horribly cute!"

Her voice boomed like a clap of thunder. More dark clouds swept in, blocking the sunlight. The air suddenly grew cold. A real clap of thunder answered the Queen's voice. Lightning flashed, and rain poured down from the clouds.

"I did not need a silly spell at all!" she boasted. "It is gray and gloomy. My frightful day is finally here!"

But the Queen's bad mood was only strong enough to cause a short storm. After a minute, the rain lightened and then stopped completely. The clouds parted, and the sun shone through. Where the sunlight hit

"Noooooo!" the Queen shrieked.

She stomped her foot, then stormed back to her room in the castle.

As she went, she wondered what else she could do to get rid of that

"Magic Mirror on the wall, tell me how to stop this all!" the Queen yelled at the Magic Mirror.

The face shimmered inside the mirror. "If Your Majesty desires gloom, then stay inside a darkened room," it replied.

"That is the most sensible thing you have said all day," the Queen snarled.

She stayed inside and sulked, leaving the cheerful fall day outside.

A SNACK FOR THE QUEEN

IT was a lovely day in Wonderland. Alice was sitting in a garden, watching the bread-and-butterflies flitter from flower to flower.

"Why, their wings look just like buttered bread!" she exclaimed. "Everything here in Wonderland is so very curious."

As Alice looked around, she heard a voice behind her.

"Oh dear, oh dear, oh dear!"

Alice turned to see the White Rabbit running through the garden. "Is everything all right?" she asked.

The White Rabbit stopped. "The Queen of Hearts is hungry, but nothing in the palace seems to satisfy her. If I don't find her a tasty treat soon, she'll have my head!"

"Perhaps I can help," Alice said. "I've never had any trouble finding something to eat in Wonderland. If we work together, I'm sure we will find something that makes the Queen happy."

The White Rabbit sighed. "I do hope you are right," he said. "I quite like my head!"

"Have you tried asking the Mad Hatter?" Alice asked. "His tea table is always filled with treats."

"Oh, no. I try to steer clear of the hatter," the White Rabbit replied. "He's always causing trouble."

"That's true," Alice said. "But it's still worth a try."

Alice started down the path to the Mad Hatter's house. Suddenly, she stopped short.

"Perhaps we don't have to visit the Mad Hatter after all," she said, studying a bush. "Look at these cupcakes! Don't they look tasty?"

Alice plucked a cupcake from the bush, and she and the White Rabbit hurried to the palace.

"There you are!" the Queen of Hearts yelled when she spied the rabbit. Then she saw Alice. "You!" she shouted. "Off with your—"

Alice didn't give the Queen a chance to finish. "We brought you a cupcake, Your Majesty," she said, handing the Queen the treat.

The Queen actually smiled. "Why, thank you," she said, reaching for it.

Before the Queen could take a bite, the cupcake began to move. Two wings opened up, and it flew away. It wasn't a cupcake at all. It was a bird!

Alice's eyes grew wide. The Queen would surely have her head now!

Alice and the White Rabbit quickly ran from the palace. They hadn't gone far when the Cheshire Cat appeared on the path in front of them.

"What's the hurry?" he asked them.

"We need to find a snack for the Queen," Alice replied.

The Cheshire Cat looked down at the berries on the bush beneath him. "Take her some of these blue berries," he suggested.

"But these aren't blueberries," Alice said. "They're red!"

"Red or blue, they're quite tasty," the Cheshire Cat said.

"The Queen is very impatient," the White Rabbit said. "And we don't have anything else to bring her. . . ."

Alice agreed. It seemed they had no choice. She and the White Rabbit picked the berries and took them to the Queen. She promptly began to gobble them down.

"Delicious!" she cried. "I suppose you may keep your heads after all!"

But then the Queen noticed something: her fingers were blue! So were her hands, and her arms. . . .

"What have you done?" she shrieked.

"Oh, dear," Alice said. "That must be why the Cheshire Cat called them *blue* berries. They look red, but they turn you blue when you eat them!"

"Fix me!" the Queen yelled.

The White Rabbit nervously tapped his paws together. "Whatever will we do?"

"I have an idea," Alice said. She ran back to the bush where they had seen the Cheshire Cat. Next to it was a bush with blue berries. She quickly picked some and hurried back to the Queen.

"Eat these!" Alice urged her.

The Queen scowled. "Why should I trust you?"

"Well, I'm just guessing," Alice replied, "but if you don't try, you'll stay blue."

The Queen frowned and ate some of the blue berries. Slowly, the blue faded from her skin.

"I suppose that worked," the Queen said. "But I'm still hungry!"

Alice and the White Rabbit hurried off to find another snack for the Queen. Soon they bumped into Tweedledum and Tweedledee. The twins were dancing and singing a silly song.

"When it comes to treats, we are not picky.

We love a treat that's sweet and sticky,

A snack you can eat when you need something quickie.

It's lollipops for us!"

Alice noticed that each one was clutching two handfuls of yummy-looking lollipops.

"Excuse me," she said. "We just happen to be looking for a tasty treat for the Queen. May we have a lollipop?"

"If it's for the Queen, we can't say no," said Tweedledum.

"So take a lollipop and go!" finished Tweedledee, handing Alice a bright red lollipop.

Alice and the White Rabbit quickly took the red lollipop to the
Queen of Hearts.

"Hmmm," said the Queen. "I *do* like lollipops. And it *is* the perfect
color. Let me give it a try."

She licked the lollipop and smiled. Then her face turned bright red
with heat.

"Spicy! Spicy!" she yelled. "Somebody bring me some water!"

While the guards rushed to help the Queen, Alice and the White
Rabbit slipped away from the palace again.

"That's it. I'm going to the Mad Hatter's house," Alice said. "I'm sure
he will have a good snack for the Queen."

"I'll wait here," the White Rabbit said.

Alice quickly made her way to the Mad Hatter's house. She found him serving tea to the March Hare.

"Excuse me," she said, "but I was wondering if you could help. The White Rabbit and I need to bring the Queen of Hearts a snack in a hurry. She's very hungry."

The March Hare's ears perked up. "The Queen, you say?" He looked at the Mad Hatter.

"Yes, I did," Alice replied.

The Mad Hatter grinned. He handed a cookie to Alice.

"This is exactly what she needs," he promised.

So Alice and the White Rabbit took the cookie to the Queen of Hearts. She sniffed it.

"It smells good," she said, frowning suspiciously. "And it *looks* tasty."

The Queen bit into the cookie. "It *is* tasty," she said.

Suddenly, something very strange happened. The Queen began to shrink! She got smaller and smaller until she was almost the size of the cookie.

"Guards! Guards! Off with their heads!" she yelled. But her voice was so tiny and squeaky that the guards didn't hear her.

Alice and the White Rabbit hurried away.

"The Mad Hatter was right," Alice said with a giggle. "That cookie is exactly what the Queen needed!"

CORAL FESTIVAL CHAOS

Ursula the sea witch was always grumpy. But that day she was in an especially foul mood. She was deep in her lair with Flotsam and Jetsam. "What day is it today?" she called to the eels.

"It's the beginning of the Coral Festival," Flotsam and Jetsam said in unison.

It was time for King Triton's annual Coral Festival, when all the merpeople gathered together to celebrate the beauty and splendor of the ocean's coral.

The merfolk loved the festival, but Ursula despised the celebration. "Too much joy," complained the villainess.

Ursula peered through her crystal ball and scowled as she watched King Triton welcome his guests.

"How kind of you all to join us. My daughters and I have a fun-filled festival planned for you."

The merfolk cheered and clapped for the exciting day ahead.

"I can't wait for the race," exclaimed one mermaid.

"My favorite event is the water ballet," another chimed in.

"Nothing beats the parade," said a third.

"Know what would make me happy?" sneered Ursula. "Making those cheery merpeople *un*happy."

"Flotsam! Jetsam! We've got a Coral Festival
to spoil, starting with that silly sea race." She
whispered her plan to her eels, and they swam
off toward Atlantica.

King Triton and all his merfolk friends
gathered outside the castle gates to watch the
race. Little did they know Ursula and her
minions were watching, too.

One, two, three . . . the merpeople swam by at amazing speeds! They swam around rocks and between coral, racing for the finish line. But Ursula was ready for them. She hid behind the biggest rock and waited.

As they passed, Ursula stretched out her mighty tentacles and thrashed them, hoping to scare off the merfolk.

But the giant wave only helped the racers swim faster.

The merpeople clapped and cheered for the winners of the race. Ursula watched in frustration as King Triton awarded trophies to them. But she had more tricks up her sleeve.

"Not to worry. I have an even better idea," Ursula said with a cackle, noticing the dancers in the distance. "We're going to wreck the water ballet."

So Ursula, Flotsam, and Jetsam snuck into the concert hall, where the orchestra played a soft, soothing tune. Onstage, the mermaid ballerinas spun, swayed, and sashayed in sync with the music.

Ursula snickered. "These poor unfortunate dancers are about to lose their rhythm."

She placed a record on the phonograph. The record's loud rock music drowned out the sound of the symphony. "Now the Coral Festival will be spoiled for sure," she sneered.

As the new beat filled the concert hall, all the dancers looked at each other, confused. Then one by one everyone began to catch on. The dancers started rocking out to the brand-new song.

In her hiding place, Ursula frowned.

Once again, Ursula's evil plan had backfired. The audience tapped their fins to the catchy beat and cheered on the dancers.

"Those cheery merfolk are enjoying the Coral Festival more than ever," harrumphed Ursula as she shattered the phonograph records.

That's when Ursula saw King Triton swoosh by. "Of course—it's time for the parade!" she cried with an evil twinkle in her eye. "That's how I'll spoil the festival!

"We'll build our own float and join the procession," she plotted. "The merfolk will be so scared when I appear! Oh, my, this is going to be fun!"

The parade route wound through a glorious reef covered in coral.
All the merfolk gathered around to watch in awe.

They applauded as the floats went by carrying the champions of the race and the dancers, who all waved as they passed.

Ursula hurried to join the parade, but the finale began before
she could catch up. All the colorful coral opened, creating a brilliant
spectacle that blocked the sea witch's way.

The merfolk oohed and aahed at the vibrant colors. They all agreed that this had been the best Coral Festival yet.

"No!" Ursula cried. She had failed to spoil any of the fun at the Coral Festival. The merpeople were happier than ever. In the foulest mood, Ursula rode away on her float, back to her lair to form her next evil plan.

Peter Pan

CAPTAIN HOOK'S SHADOW

"**W**alk the plank, Peter Pan!" John Darling yelled, waving a wooden sword at his brother, Michael. The boys were playing in the nursery. John was pretending to be Captain Hook, and Michael was pretending to be Peter Pan.

"I *won't* walk the plank," Michael said, "and you're a codfish, Captain Hook!"

"I'll get you for that, Pan!" John cried.

As the brothers chased each other around the room, Michael felt like he was back in Never Land.

"All right, John and Michael, time for bed," Wendy said, walking into the room.

"Just five more minutes?" John pleaded.

"All right," Wendy agreed. "A few more minutes."

John and Michael began another pretend battle. But the minutes passed quickly, and soon Wendy returned. "Now it's really time for bed, you two," she said.

Michael and John put down their swords and crawled into their beds. Wendy turned out the light and got into bed, too. She was sleeping in the nursery while her new bedroom was being decorated.

Michael pulled up the covers. He wasn't the least bit tired.

Soon John and Wendy were fast asleep. Michael squeezed his eyes shut, but it was no use. He kept picturing Captain Hook trying to capture Peter Pan.

Suddenly, Michael heard a rattling sound, followed by a loud *whoosh!*

He opened his eyes and looked around. The nursery windows were wide open, but no one was there.

Then Michael noticed a shadow against the far wall. He gasped in fear. The shadow looked just like Captain Hook!

Michael wanted to run, but he couldn't. He would have to hide.

Michael quickly dove under the covers. Captain Hook was scary! But being under the covers didn't make Michael feel any safer. He needed to know if the pirate was in the nursery.

Slowly, he lifted the bottom edge of his blanket and peeked out.

Michael still couldn't see Hook, but the captain's shadow was right there against the wall—as large as life. The shadow looked around the nursery for a moment. Then it began to creep toward the far corner.

A chill ran down Michael's spine.

Captain Hook was headed right toward Wendy!

Michael knew he had to protect Wendy. As he glanced around the nursery, his eyes fell on his wooden sword.

Michael reached down and grabbed the sword just as the shadow got to Wendy. He threw off his covers and leaped toward it.

The shadow stumbled backward. Michael lunged at it again, but it swiped at him with its hook.

Michael dove under his bed. The shadow reached for him, but he darted away just in time.

The shadow jumped onto the bed. Michael gulped, waiting for the hook to swipe at him again. He wondered why he was seeing only Captain Hook's shadow. Where was Hook hiding?

Michael knew he had to do something. He couldn't stay under the bed forever. Captain Hook was sure to get him sooner or later.

Michael dashed into the middle of the room, but the shadow chased him. As he tried to get away, he tripped over a ball.

The shadow skulked toward him. Shivering, Michael pictured the crocodile that waited for anyone who walked the plank.

Suddenly, Michael heard someone call out, *"Cock-a-doodle-doo!"*

"Peter Pan!" Michael shouted as his hero flew in. "I'm so glad you're here! Captain Hook tried to get Wendy, but I stopped him."

"Hook is here?" Peter asked, looking around.

"Why, it's Captain Hook's shadow," Peter said. "Don't let it get away!"

The shadow tried to run, but Peter flew after it.

"It's only a shadow?" Michael asked. Suddenly, he wasn't as scared. He leaped up from the floor and ran after it, too.

"Grab it from the other side!" Peter called.

Michael ran toward the shadow from the right as Peter flew at it from the left. The shadow was trapped! In a flash, Michael reached out and caught it.

"Put it in here!" Peter cried, holding out a sack.

Michael stuffed the shadow into the sack, and Peter tied it closed.

"That was close," Peter said.

"Why was Captain Hook's shadow here?" Michael asked.

"I stole the shadow for a prank," Peter explained. "Some prank! The shadow has been nothing but trouble. It pulled the Lost Boys' tails and put pine cones in their beds. And then it flew away from Never Land to cause trouble in London."

"That sounds really awful!" Michael cried, looking at Peter with wide eyes. "I'm glad we caught it!"

Peter nodded. "Thanks for all your help, Michael! I've got to get back to Never Land.

"Do you want to come with me?" Peter asked Michael. "It'll be a great adventure!"

"Not without Wendy and John," Michael replied.

"Then let's bring them!" Peter said, flying to Wendy's bed. He reached down to give her a gentle shake, then drew his hand back. "Aw, she's fast asleep." He looked at John and said, "John's asleep, too."

"Maybe next time," Peter said, jumping to the window ledge. "Goodbye, Michael. Tell Wendy and John that I said hello!" he called. Then he flew out into the night.

"I will!" Michael promised. He waved good night and then went back to bed, smiling. He was glad to have had another adventure with Peter.

Disney
Sleeping Beauty

A MESSAGE FOR MALEFICENT

IT was a time of celebration. King Stefan was getting married!

The king's subjects rejoiced. But no one was happier than the three good fairies, Flora, Fauna, and Merryweather. They hurried to the castle to help the king and his future bride.

Princess Leah had many ideas for her wedding, but she did not know whom to invite. She wanted to make sure no one in the kingdom was missed; so she asked the good fairies to make and deliver the invitations.

"Blue wedding invitations!" Merryweather said. "Can you think of anything lovelier?" With a flick of her wand she created a stack of blue envelopes.

"Oh, no, that won't do. They should be pink!" Flora said, changing the envelopes to a pale pink.

Back and forth the envelopes went, until at last they settled on a light purple that both fairies had to agree was quite nice.

On the other side of the room, Fauna was hard at work on the guest list. "We don't need to invite too many people," she said.

Flora looked up. "Do you think we should invite . . ." Her voice trailed off.

"Maleficent?" Merryweather asked. The fairy Maleficent lived high on the Forbidden Mountain. Her presence rarely brought any good cheer, but still, she *was* one of the king's subjects.

With a sigh, Fauna nodded. "I suppose we must," she said.

Merryweather shuddered. Just thinking about Maleficent gave her the shivers. "Who will we get to deliver the invitation?" she asked. "The way to Maleficent's castle is treacherous, and we cannot risk the invitation getting lost."

"One of us will have to go," Flora said. She flicked her hand and a dove appeared from her wand. It circled the room three times and then landed on Merryweather's shoulder. It was up to her to deliver the invitation to Maleficent!

The next day Merryweather set off for Maleficent's castle. By
evening she had reached the woods around the Forbidden Mountain.
Her magic was weak there. She would have to walk.
    Merryweather looked at a winding path that led into the woods.

It was getting dark, and the wind moaned eerily through the trees. Shivering, Merryweather pulled her wand out of her cloak pocket. With a flick of her wrist, she lit the wand. The warm light comforted her, and she bravely continued on the path.

Alas, Merryweather was not alone in the woods. Maleficent's minions, the goons, were out patrolling. Even worse for poor Merryweather, the evil creatures loved causing mischief.

"I'll be there soon. Everything will be fine," Merryweather told herself as she tried to take her mind off the spookiness of the dark woods. But as she went around a curve in the path, three of the goons jumped out at her.

Screaming, Merryweather ran down the path as fast as her little
legs would carry her. Finally, she lost the goons.

"Those wicked creatures!" she said when she had calmed down.
"I'd like to scare *them* and see how they'd like it!"

Merryweather looked around. Somehow, it seemed the woods had
grown even darker. A cold wind blew through the trees, chilling the
little fairy to the core. Merryweather wanted nothing more than to
turn back, but the other fairies were counting on her.

As Merryweather made her way down the path, she noticed the trees growing closer and closer together. Large thorns stuck out from the trunks, making it impossible to get through without a scratch.

"Oh, fiddlesticks!" she yelled as her cloak caught on a thorn. Merryweather freed herself from the tree and hurried away as carefully as she could.

The sooner she delivered the invitation, the sooner she could get back to the bright, warm castle.

Finally, Merryweather reached the edge of the woods. A giant stone staircase loomed above her, leading to Maleficent's lair.

Up, up, up Merryweather climbed until at last she came to a
rickety bridge. On the other side was Maleficent's castle. Its jagged
peaks rose into the sky, and a dark storm cloud circled overhead.

Merryweather looked nervously at the bridge. It seemed like it could collapse at any moment. Tucking the invitation into her cloak, she stepped onto the bridge. The wood shook and creaked with every step the little fairy took. Merryweather kept her eyes on the stone landing ahead of her. Below her was a deep chasm. If the bridge gave out, she would have a long way to fall.

Finally, Merryweather reached the other side. As she stepped onto the landing, a blast of green magic burst out of Maleficent's castle and a loud scream filled the air!

That was the last straw for Merryweather. She took out the invitation and carefully placed it on the castle's doorstep. Then she raced back across the bridge, down the steps, and through the woods. She was so busy running away, she didn't see the goons who had been following her pick up the invitation and scamper off with it!

Merryweather didn't stop until she reached King Stefan's castle. She found Flora and Fauna in the great hall.

"Why, Merryweather, dear, whatever is the matter?" Flora asked.

"Maleficent had better come to this wedding," Merryweather said

when she had caught her breath. "The journey to deliver the invitation nearly scared me to death!"

Flora smiled at Merryweather. "Come now," she said. "How bad could it really have been?"

Soon the day of King Stefan and Princess Leah's wedding arrived. Everyone in the kingdom gathered for the happy event. Everyone, that is, except for Maleficent.

From high on the Forbidden Mountain, the fairy gazed down on the celebration. "Look at those fools," she said. "Who do they think they are, not inviting me to their celebration? Well, enjoy it while you can. I'll get you for this . . . someday."

Disney
THE LION KING

A DARK AND SCAR-Y NIGHT

Scar sighed, watching the afternoon sun sink lower in the sky.

"Oh, Scar!" someone called. It was Mufasa's steward, Zazu. "I bring an important announcement from the king!"

"And what, pray tell, does Mufasa want?" Scar asked.

"*King* Mufasa," Zazu said, correcting him, "has decided it is time to prepare Simba for his future reign. This evening he would like you to tell him tales of kings past—a family story time, as it were."

Sensing Scar's anger, Zazu made a quick exit. "Story time begins promptly at sundown!" he called.

Scar grinned as a positively wicked idea began to creep its way into his mind.

Scar slunk over to the Elephant Graveyard. If his plan was going to work, he would need the help of the hyenas.

"So let me get this straight," Shenzi said. "You want us to sneak into the lions' den and take the cub? With Mufasa right *there*?"

Scar smiled. "Leave Mufasa to me. And once you steal the hair ball, you can have him."

By the time Scar and the three hyenas reached the Pride Lands, night had fallen.

"Now remember," Scar growled, "listen closely to my story. I will let you know when and how to strike!"

Before the hyenas could reply, they heard the sound of voices coming toward them.

"Go!" Scar whispered as he spotted Mufasa and Simba rounding the corner.

"Scar," Mufasa said, "Simba and I were headed up to begin the storytelling."

"As was I," Scar replied quickly. "I think I've got a *very* good tale to tell, too."

Simba cocked his head. "Is it scary? I wanna hear something *really* scary. Not some boring story about an old king."

Scar knelt down, an evil glint in his eye. "The scariest."

"Cool!" Simba cried.

Soon the lions had gathered. Simba's friend Nala sat beside him. Across from them, Mufasa greeted the pride.

"Who would like to begin?" Mufasa asked.

"I would be honored to—" Zazu started.

"I'll go first," Scar interrupted, stepping forward. Mufasa looked at his brother in surprise.

"He said he had a *really* scary story," Simba whispered to Nala.

"Very well," Mufasa said. "Scar, the floor is yours."

Scar took a deep breath and began: "Once upon a time, there lived a foolish king with many enemies. One night, the king decided to host a gathering. He invited animals from far and wide. His enemies knew the king would be distracted by his guests. This was their chance!

"The king's enemies invited some mighty elephants to the gathering. The elephants kicked up a large amount of dirt." Scar scraped his paws on the ground, creating a cloud of dust.

Scar continued: "This made it difficult for everyone to see. It was the perfect opportunity to take the king without anyone noticing."

Hearing their cue, the hyenas snuck toward the distracted lions, who were squinting at Scar through the haze. They had almost reached Simba when . . .

"Ah-choo!" Simba sneezed, diverting everyone's attention to him. The hyenas sprinted out of sight.

"Perhaps that's enough dust, Scar," Mufasa advised.

"Of course," Scar drawled, his eyes darkening.

"But things did not go as planned," Scar continued. "The king's enemies soon came up with another idea. One night, when everyone was fast asleep, they snuck into the king's den, covered in mud to disguise themselves. When the king woke, he didn't know his enemies were there." He raised his voice pointedly. *"Right there with him. Disguised."*

The hyenas—looking as though they had rolled around in the mud—inched toward Simba on their stomachs.

Suddenly, Mufasa stood up. The hyenas gasped at the sight of the mighty lion and made another hasty retreat.

Frowning, the king peered through the darkness. "Hmmm . . . I thought I heard something." He sat down again. "I apologize, Scar."

"Yes, well . . ." Scar went on, clearly agitated. "The enemies' second idea to sabotage the king did not work, either. So they had to resort to their third and final plan.

"Each day, the king stood on a great rock very similar to this one, and made announcements to his subjects.

"So his enemies gathered at the *base* of the rock," Scar continued. "They climbed up one another until the enemy at the top was just high enough to reach the king's paws. And then . . ."

Scar paused as the hyenas climbed up to reach the space just beneath Simba.

"THEY POUNCED ON THE KING!" Scar bellowed.

The lions were startled, but Scar's outcry had also scared the three hyenas! They tumbled down the face of Pride Rock.

Out of the corner of his eye, Scar saw the dazed and bruised hyenas shuffling back toward the Elephant Graveyard. He sighed.

"What happened next?" Simba asked.

"Then the king swatted the enemies away," Scar said. "The end."

Simba looked disappointed. "Uncle Scar," he said, "that was a nice story, but maybe next time you could make it a little scarier!"

FORTUNE-TELLER FIASCO

Jafar and his parrot, Iago, were shopping in Agrabah's bazaar.

"Do you see what I see?" Jafar asked the bird.

"Lunch?" Iago said, eyeing a table full of apples.

"Better," Jafar said. "It's Farah the fortune-teller. Farah sees the future in her crystal ball. She can tell you exactly what will happen in your life. I must get my future read, Iago."

"Welcome, Jafar," Farah said. "Welcome, Iago."

"Hold it right there," Iago squawked. "How did you know our names?"

"My crystal ball knows all," Farah said. "It's magical."

"We've come to hear our futures," Jafar told Farah.

The crystal ball glowed brightly. "How interesting," Farah said.

"What do you see?" Jafar asked.

Farah looked deep into her crystal ball. "Soon Iago will have the lunch of his dreams."

"What about *my* future?" Jafar asked.

"Like you've always wished, Jafar, fame and attention will befall you. And so will—"

"*Fortune!*" Jafar said, cutting Farah off. "I always knew I'd have fame and fortune! I'm going to be rich, rich, rich."

Jafar began to cackle, drowning out the rest of Farah's words.

Jafar looked at his snake staff and then at Iago.

"I need that magical crystal ball for myself," Jafar whispered to Iago. "I need to know exactly how I will be getting all these riches."

"Oh, boy," Iago said. "Please don't tell me you have an evil plan."

"I have an evil plan." Jafar said.

"Of course you do," Iago said.

Jafar held up his snake staff. Its eyes glowed red, hypnotizing Farah. "You will give me your crystal ball!" Jafar ordered.

"Give . . . you . . . my . . . crystal . . . ball . . ." Farah repeated Jafar's
command, seemingly in a daze. Farah picked up her glowing ball
from the table. She handed it to Jafar. . . .

But right when he took it, the crystal ball bounced out of his grip.
"That ball has a mind of its own," Jafar said. The ball rolled off,
disappearing into the surrounding crowd.
"Find that crystal ball, Iago!" Jafar screeched.

"I'd rather find my dream lunch," Iago said.

But he did as he was ordered and flew after it above the mob. "It went that way," Iago called down.

Jafar wove through tables and ducked under a camel. "I see it," Jafar panted. "Over by that monkey!" He dove for the crystal ball. "I've got it! I've—oops."

The ball rolled out of reach, and Jafar crashed into the monkey instead.

"Tharg barrrg mern!" Jafar shouted.

"Oh, boy," Iago said. "Jafar has officially gone nuts."

Jafar spit out a mouthful of monkey fur. "I said, 'That ball is mine'!"

Jafar chased the ball over sand dunes and through caves and back to the bazaar. The bazaar was so crowded that the ball had to slow to a stop.

"I've got you now," Jafar said.

He lunged for the ball once more, but it bounced up high. "Not again," Jafar groaned as he crashed into a table stacked with apples.

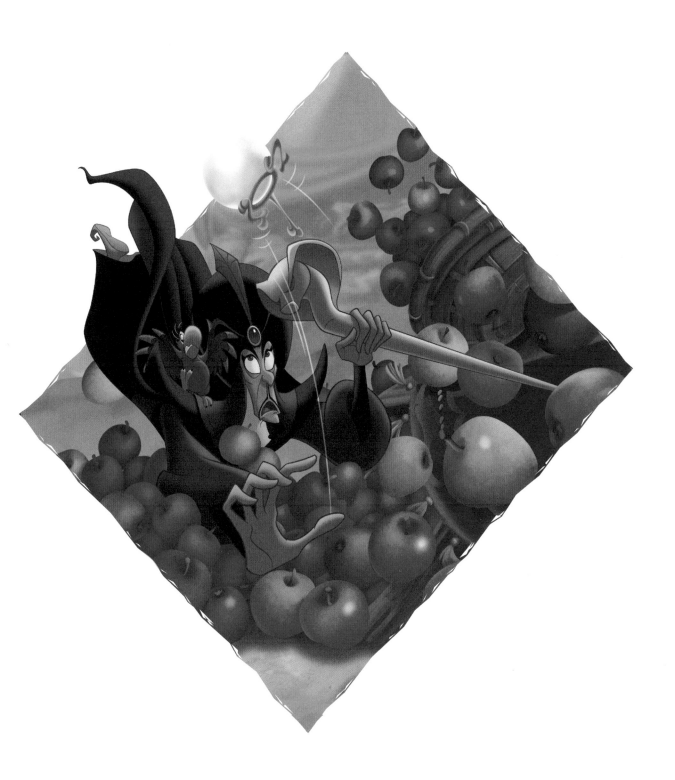

Hundreds of apples rained down, burying Jafar and Iago. "I'm drowning in fruit!" Jafar shrieked.

The bazaar filled with laughter. "Jafar will be famous for this," a woman said.

"Help me, Iago," Jafar ordered.

But Iago was too busy eating his way through the apples. "Farah was right," he squawked. "This is the lunch of my dreams."

Jafar was tripping over apples, struggling to get to his feet, when he saw Farah standing in front of him.

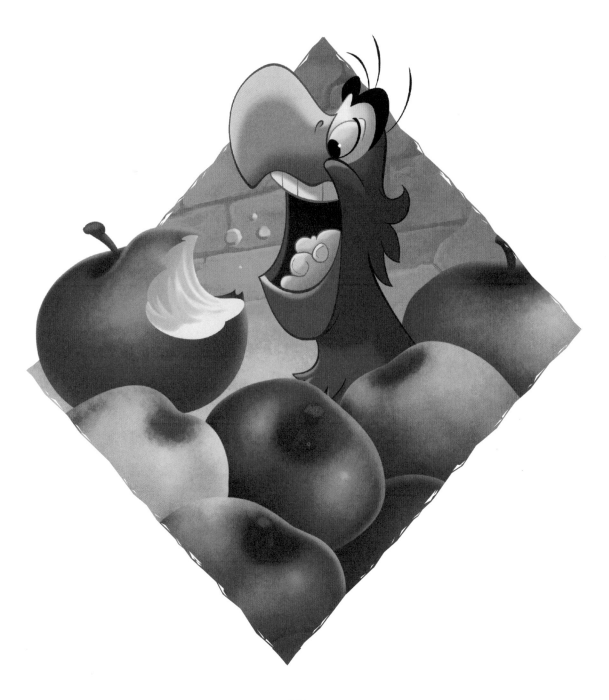

Suddenly, Jafar heard a loud crack from under the pile of apples.

"My snake staff," he gasped.

If his snake staff was broken, then Farah was no longer hypnotized.

Jafar fought his way out of the pile.

"Where's the fame and fortune you promised me?" Jafar demanded.

"Look around. You have plenty of fame," Farah said with a laugh.
"But I never said you'd have fortune. In fact, you didn't let me finish
telling you what I saw in my crystal ball."

"W-what . . ." Jafar stuttered.

Farah cleared her throat, "As you've always wished, Jafar, fame and attention will befall you. And so will . . . hundreds of apples!"

All the people at the bazaar laughed at Jafar. Iago continued to feast on his best lunch ever.